# THE
# Worst Princess

For Guinevere, Niamh, Emelia, Annabel, Esther, Elise, Esme, Martha, Orla and rebel princesses everywhere – AK

For Freya and Molly – SO

**SIMON AND SCHUSTER**
First published in Great Britain in 2012 by Simon and Schuster UK Ltd
1st Floor, 222 Gray's Inn Road, London WC1X 8HB
A CBS Company

Text copyright © 2012 Anna Kemp
Illustrations copyright © 2012 Sara Ogilvie

ISBN: 978-1-84738-875-9 (HB)
ISBN: 978-1-84738-876-6 (PB)
Printed in China
10 9 8 7 6 5

# THE Worst Princess

Anna Kemp ◆ Sara Ogilvie

**SIMON AND SCHUSTER**

London   New York   Sydney   Toronto   New Delhi

**Once upon a time,** in a tower near you,
Lived a lonely princess – the Princess Sue.

"Some day," she sighed, "my prince will come,
But I wish he'd move his royal bum.

I've waited for a hundred years,
I'm getting stiff, I'm bored to tears.

I've read the books,
I know the score,
I've grown my plaits
down to the floor.
I really need to get some air,
To see the world
and cut my hair."

Then . . .

. . . Just as Sue was about to scream,
A prince appeared, 'twas like a dream.

"Oh, Princess, pretty as a pea!
I've journeyed far to rescue thee."

"I fought, I won,

I shocked, I awed.

You should have seen me swing my sword.
I've slain all kinds of vicious foe . . ."

"That's fab," said Sue. "Now can we go?
Your true love's kiss should do the trick,
So pucker up and kiss me quick!"

They charged off on a dashing steed.
"Whoopee!" cried Sue. "At last! I'm freed!
Today I start my happy end!"

But then she saw around the bend . . .

. . . "Where are we going, my prince, my love?"

"Back to my castle, turtle dove.
My perfect peach, my precious flower,
You have a penthouse in the tower."

"I'd rather ride a horse," said Sue,
"And do all kinds of fun stuff too!"

"Too bad," said Prince. "You know the rules. Didn't you listen at Princess School?

It's me who wears the armour here,
And you wear dresses, are we clear?

Just smile a lot and twist your curls.
Dragon-bashing's not for girls."

Alone in her tower, Sue started to spit,
"What a disaster, my prince is a twit!"

Then in the skies she suddenly spied . . .

A fearsome dragon with flashing eyes.

Sue didn't run, she had no fear.
Instead, she had a bright idea.

"Hey you!" she called, "with the scary claws,
Fancy some tea for your fiery jaws?"
"Ooh, yes," said Dragon. "What a relief,
That pesky prince is giving me grief."

"Me too," said Sue. "The sneaky rascal
has locked me in this stupid castle."

"The rotter!" gasped Dragon. "That just won't do!
We need to teach him a thing or two!"
The dragon sniffed some nasal spray . . .

... Then blew the tower clean away!

"Princess Sue! That's quite enough!"
The prince was back, and in a huff.
"Where's your tower? Just look at your dress!
You really are the worst princess.

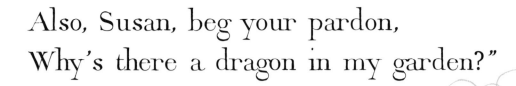

Also, Susan, beg your pardon,
Why's there a dragon in my garden?"

"Perhaps I am the worst princess,"
Laughed Princess Sue. "My hair's a mess.
My tower's a wreck, but I don't care,
I've booked a flight with Dragon-Air!"

The dragon sniffed, then with two snorts . . .

...Set alight the princely shorts!

From that day on, the new-found friends toured the land from end to end.

Making mischief left and right . . .

For royal twits and naughty knights.

"You know," said Sue, as they drank their tea,
"We're a great team, you and me."
The dragon's belly shook with laughter.

**And they both lived happily ever after.**